# The Pike
## and the
# Sea Fish

Once, there was a Pike fish who lived in the river.

He was a large fish who was very proud of himself.

One day, a strong current carried him into the sea.

There he saw that he was much larger than the Sea Fishes.

He started boasting about himself and his family.

He would laugh at the Sea Fishes and feel good about himself.

He said to the Fishes, "Look how small you are.

Look at me. I am big and I am a Pike! And I am great!"

This annoyed all the little Fishes, but they kept quiet.

They did not react and kept busy with their work.

One day, a small Sea Fish got tired of hearing the Pike speak thus.

He said, "You may be bigger than me and proud of your size. But

let me tell you, if I ever reach the market, I will be sold at a much higher

price than you. I may be small, but I am worth my weight in gold!"

Being big does not always mean that you are invaluable.

## Key Words

| | |
|---|---|
| current | boasting |
| annoyed | proud |
| great | tired |